DC SUPER-PETS!™

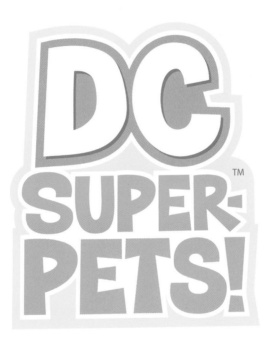

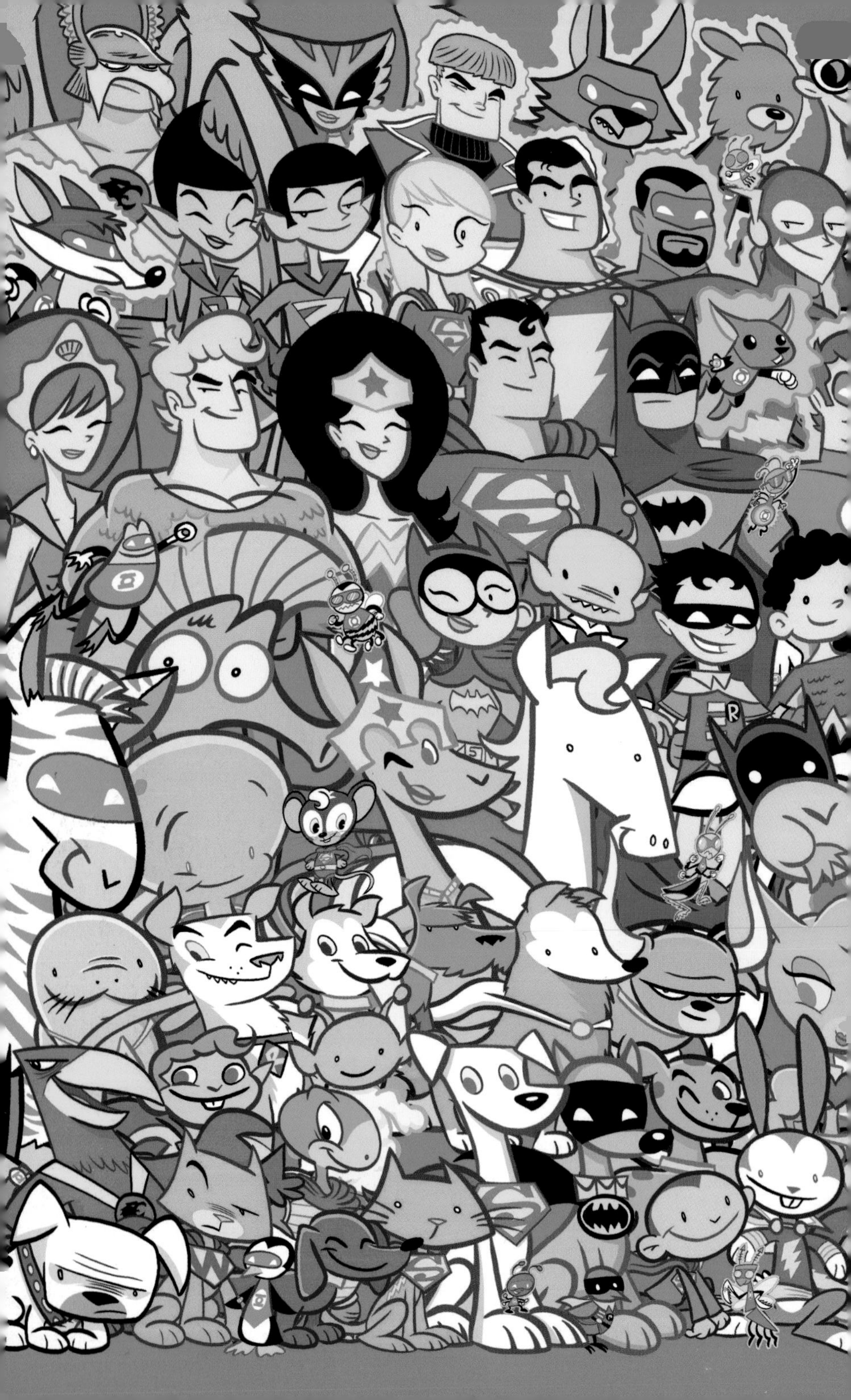

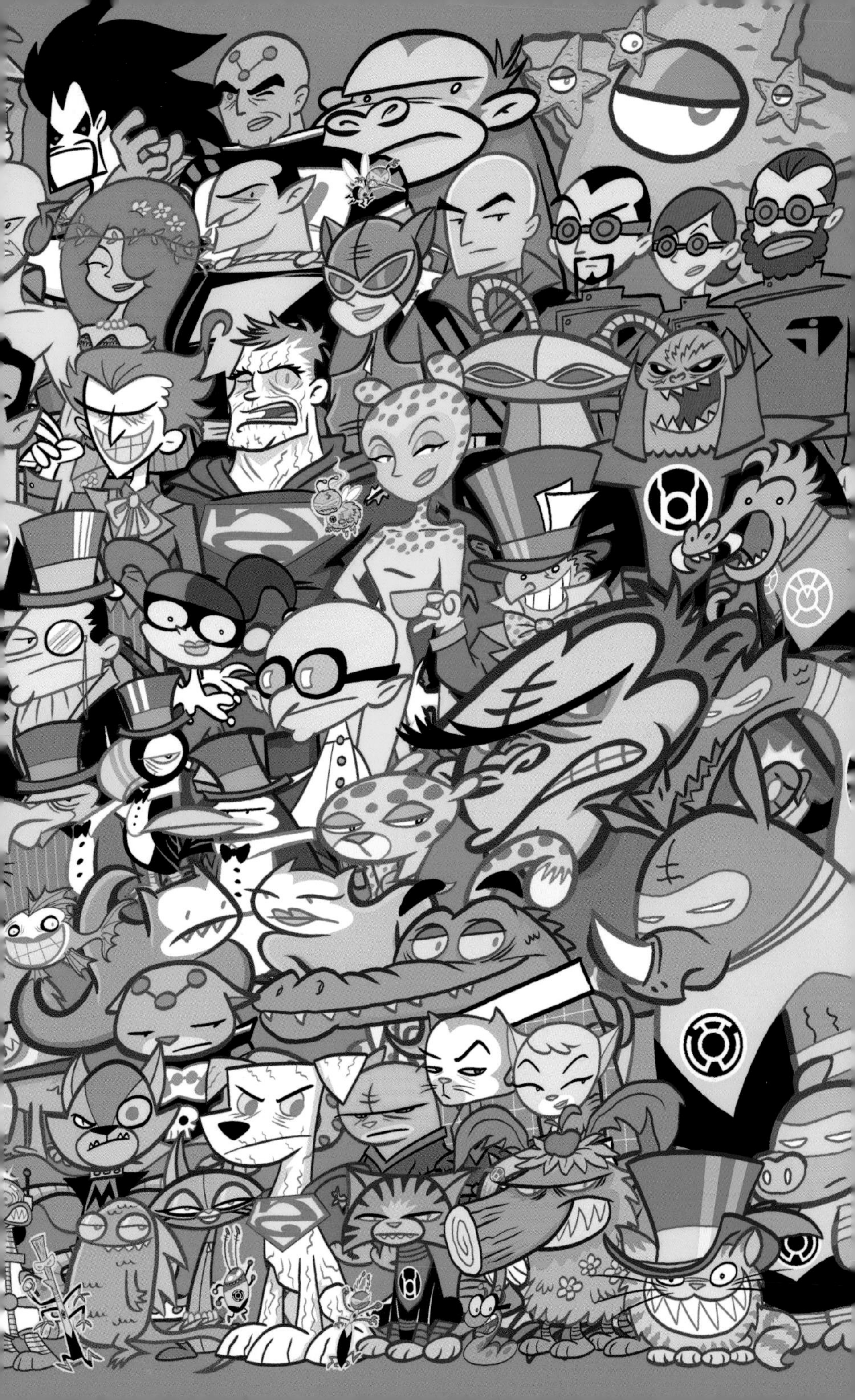

DC SUPER-PETS!™

by Sarah Hines Stephens

SLEEPY TIME CRIME

illustrated by
Art Baltazar

Superman created by
Jerry Siegel and Joe Shuster

Picture Window Books™
a capstone imprint

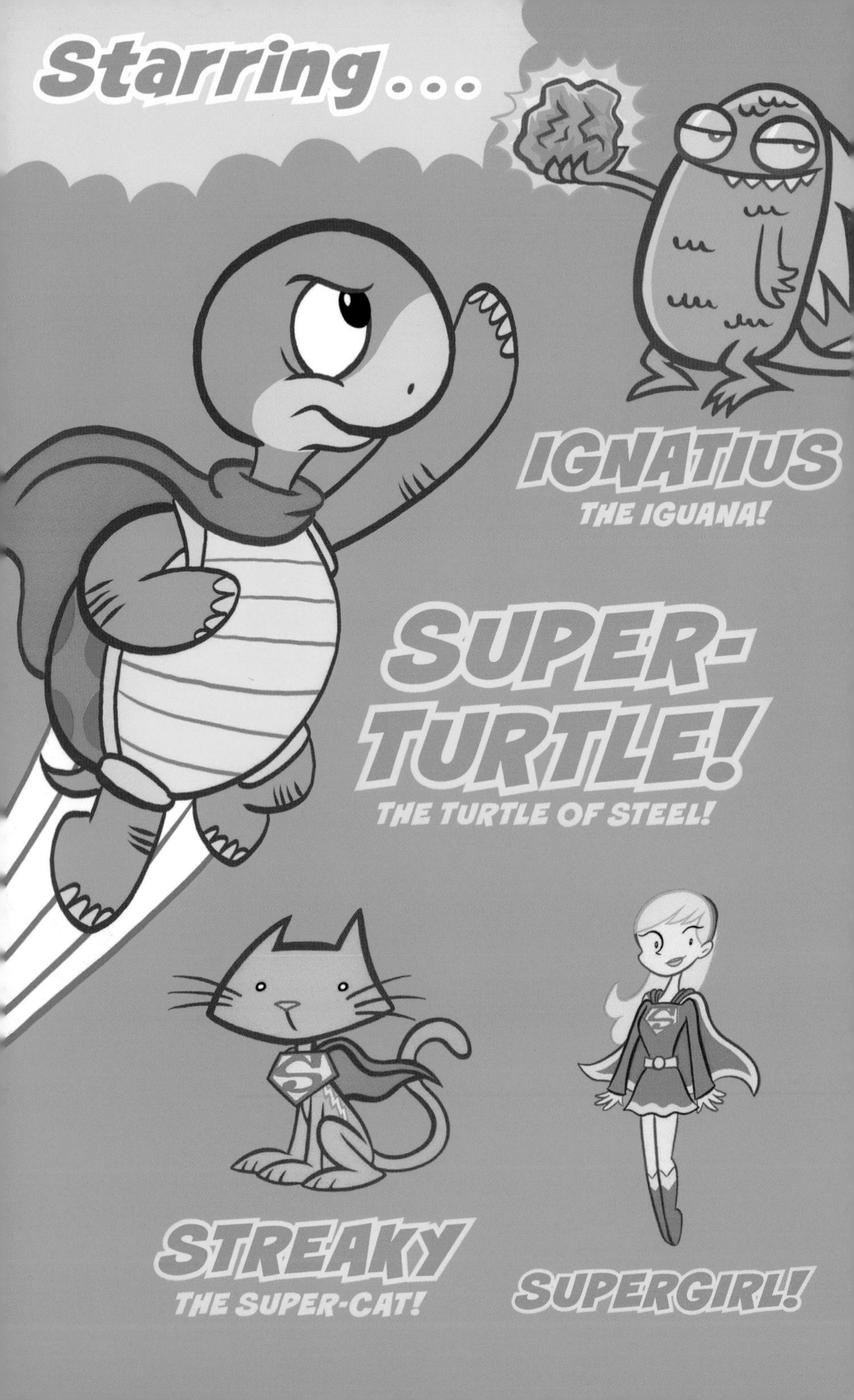
Starring . . .
IGNATIUS
THE IGUANA!
SUPER-
TURTLE!
THE TURTLE OF STEEL!
STREAKY
THE SUPER-CAT!
SUPERGIRL!

TABLE OF CONTENTS!

SUPER-TURTLE

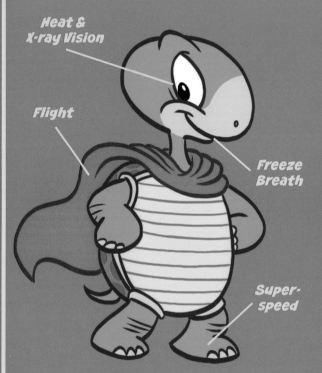

Heat &
X-ray Vision

Flight

Freeze
Breath

Super-
speed

Super Hero Owner:
SUPERMAN

Species: Turtle

Place of Birth: Krypton

Weakness: Kryptonite

Favorite Food:
Turtle treats

Bio: As Superman's pet reptile, Super-Turtle has the same superpowers as his heroic master.

Super-Pet Enemy File 016:
IGNATIUS

Wicked Smart

Kryptonite

Cold-blooded

Super-villain Owner:
LEX LUTHOR

Chapter 1

CATNAP CAPER

Supergirl yawned and stretched. She got out of bed, ready for another day of fighting crime.

The super hero looked around for her Super-Cat, **Streaky.** "Where's my little Cat of Steel?" she called.

Like most cats, Streaky was active at night. After dark, he liked to prowl the streets in search of thugs and thieves while the rest of the world slept.

Well, usually . . .

Today, Supergirl found the crime-fighting cat in the kitchen. He was curled up on a huge pile of Kitty Krunchalongs, snoring and dreaming of food. His tummy was bulging. He looked like he hadn't moved for hours.

"Streaky," Supergirl called to him again. Streaky's left ear twitched, but he didn't wake up. He was fast asleep.

"Big night with the bad guys?" Supergirl asked, patting her sleepy cat.

Then Supergirl slid Streaky to the

side. **WHOOSH!** The super hero

spun around and around at incredible

speed, creating a small whirlwind. The

Kitty Krunchalongs swirled into the air

and then back into the bag.

MEOOWWW!

Streaky was awake and ready for a snack.

"I thought you'd had enough," said Supergirl. She grabbed the bag and poured another bowl full.

"There," she said with a yawn. She placed it on the floor. "I don't know why I feel so tired," she said shaking her head and yawning again. "Maybe I didn't sleep well last night."

Sleep. Streaky loved sleep. Lately, the Super-Cat couldn't get enough.

He daydreamed about catnaps as he chewed his Kitty Krunchalongs. Streaky had only been awake for a few minutes, but all he wanted was  to grab a bite and get back to bed.

After a few more bites, Streaky curled up in a warm patch of sun. Then he heard a tapping at the door.

"Who's bothering me now?" he said.

It was **Super-Turtle!**

The powerful pet had come to see what was going on with his friend. Word on the street was that rodent robbers no longer had anything to fear in Streaky's neighborhood.

Crime was up, and criminals were laughing at the thought of the sleepy Super-Cat coming after them.

When Super-Turtle heard the rumors, he suspected something was wrong. The Streaky he knew would never allow criminals to run wild or robber rats to tease him!

As soon as he was inside, Super-Turtle saw that this was not the Streaky he knew at all. **Something was wrong . . . very wrong.**

The orange cat sat down on the mat before Super-Turtle was all the way in the door.

"Don't talk. Sleeping," Streaky mumbled. A moment later he was snoring. ZZZZZZZZZ!

"Wake up!" Super-Turtle tried shaking the sleeping cat. It was no use. Whatever the problem was, it was clear Super-Turtle was going to have to get to the bottom of it by himself.

He turned and . . .

MOOOOOSH!

Super-Turtle stepped on something soft. He bent over to take a closer look. Whatever it was had been turned to reddish goo under his foot. The reptile hero sniffed at the slime.

SNIFF! It smelled like cat food, but there was something else. Super-Turtle was picking up an evil scent.

Super-Turtle yawned. Leaning against the bag of cat food, he looked over at the dozing cat.

Suddenly, a nap seemed like a good idea to him, too. If he took a quick nap then he might be able to identify the smell. Or perhaps it would come to him later. Tomorrow. Or maybe never. Super-Turtle pulled his head into his shell. He started to sleep when . . .

Super-Turtle's eyes opened wide. This was no time for sleeping. It was no time for hiding, either. Super-Turtle had a job to do! And the suspect was in plain sight.

In a flash of green, Super-Turtle raced across the kitchen. He flung open the cupboard door, grabbed the suspect, and wrestled it to the ground.

He had defeated . . . the bag of cat food! Flipping the bag over, Super-Turtle spotted something fishy. The logo looked like LexCorp's brand. But why would the super-villain Lex Luthor be making cat food? **Unless . . .**

Super-Turtle took a closer look at the bag. It read, "New Kitty Krunchalongs! A burst of secret sauce in every bite!"

Super-Turtle had never heard of this secret sauce. He wondered if that ingredient was making Streaky sleepy.

"Streaky!" Super-Turtle tried once more to shake the cat awake. "How long have you been eating this food?"

Streaky opened one eye. "Hey, get your flippers off my Krunchalongs," he said lazily. ZZZZZZZ

"Streaky, something's wrong with your food!" Super-Turtle tried to explain. It was useless. Streaky had already gone back to sleep.

Super-Turtle needed to figure out who was poisoning Streaky, how, and why. **He had to get to the bottom of this catnap caper on his own.**

Chapter 2

EVIL INGREDIENT

Moving at lightning speed and holding the large bag in his small arms, Super-Turtle took to the skies.

WHOOSH!

Below him in the streets, people blinked and rubbed their eyes.

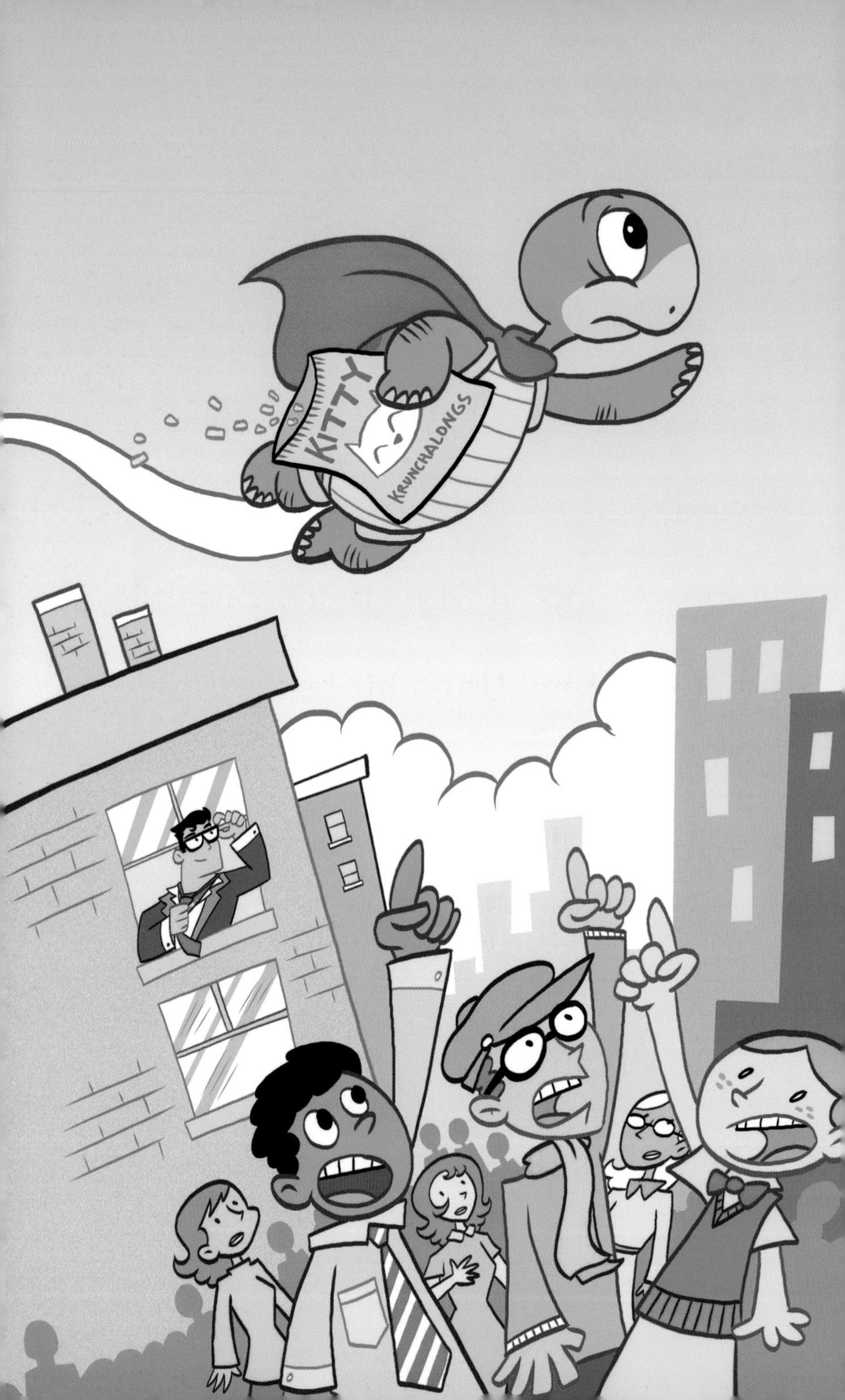
KITTY
KRUNCHALONGS

"Look up there!" the people said, pointing to the sky. "It's Super-Turtle!"

Like a discus, Super-Turtle hurtled toward the LexCorp building. The doors were locked with chains, but that didn't stop him. Using his heat vision, Super-Turtle melted the chains and broke inside.

In the building, Super-Turtle spied a scaly villain hard at work. **Ignatius Iguana!** He was dressed in a lab coat and goggles and bent over a table.

Super-Turtle flew into the air. Then he dropped the bag of Krunchalongs from the ceiling. His aim was perfect. The cat food landed directly on the evil iguana's head. SPLAT!

"Stop right there!" Super-Turtle said.

 "Curses! You spilled it all!" the

bad reptile growled. He was twisting

and flailing under the bag, trying hard

to scrape up the glowing goo that had

splattered across the floor.

"The cat's out of the bag, Ignatius.

I know you're behind the Kitty

Krunchalongs that are putting Streaky

to sleep," Super-Turtle said, swooping

closer. He only wished he knew how.

 Ignatius laughed.

"That's not all, soft shell," said
the evil lizard. "While Streaky's been
sleeping, I've prepared a little surprise
that will get that cat out of my scales
for good. In fact, he's been so busy
napping, I've even had time to come
up with a new recipe . . . for dogs!"

Super-Turtle gasped.

"That's right!" Ignatius exclaimed.
"Krypto the Super-Dog is next on
my list. But if I knew you were going
to stick your neck out, I would have
worked on some Turtle Treats first."

At that moment, Super-Turtle realized what was affecting Streaky. It was the red goo dripping from Ignatius's claws!

Suddenly, Ignatius opened his pointy fist. He flung the secret ingredient at Super-Turtle.

WOOOOSH!

Taking a quick breath, Super-Turtle ducked into his shell to avoid the glob of goo coming his way. The evil ingredient splattered all around him.

"Sweet dreams, Super-Turtle!" said Ignatius. **"Enjoy my new ingredient . . . Sleepy-Time Sauce!"**

Ignatius had stuffed Streaky's Kitty Krunchalongs with this new secret snoozing sauce. It was the reason that the Super-Cat had been eating more. It was also the reason Streaky had been sleeping more and more without ever realizing how he was changing.

Super-Turtle did not want the Sleepy-Time Sauce to change him, too.

Luckily, turtles can hold their breath for a long time. Super-Turtle could hold his for hours. Even luckier, when Super-Turtle popped his head back out, he was ready with freeze breath!

Super-Turtle froze the entire lab with a mighty blast of sub-zero air. But he had stayed in his shell too long. While Super-Turtle had been hiding, Ignatius had disappeared.

The evil lizard left a message written in the glowing goo . . .

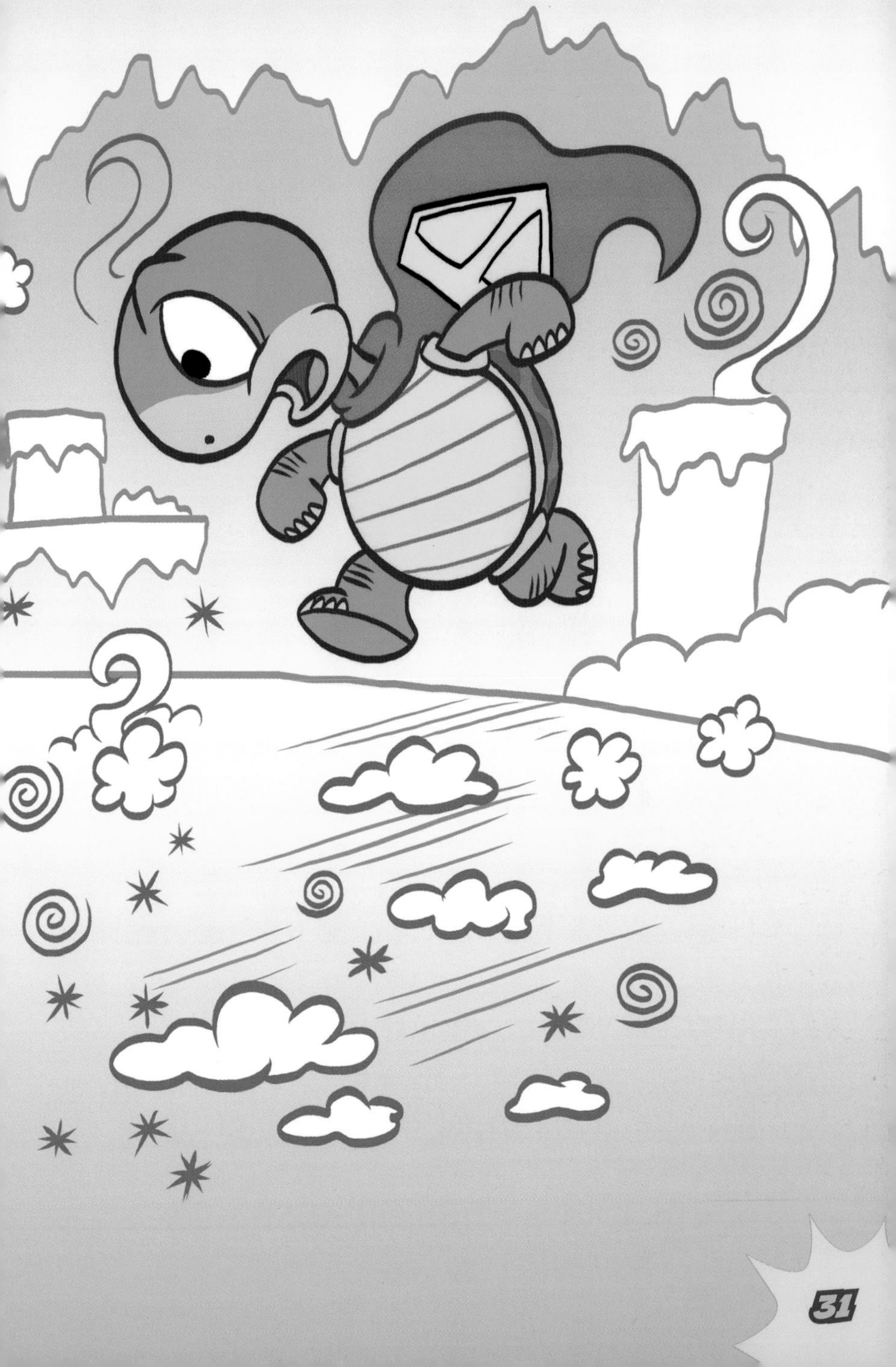

Chapter 3

LEAPING LIZARDS!

Super-Turtle flew as fast as he could to find Streaky. If he was next on the list, that meant Streaky was still first. He was on his way back to Supergirl's kitchen when something caught his eye. This must be how Ignatius planned to rid himself of Streaky!

On the roof of the LexCorp building was a giant rocket set to launch. On board was a lifetime supply of Sleepy-Time Sauce and . . . **Streaky!** The Super-Cat was still fast asleep.

Super-Turtle flew down next to the rocket's boosters. An awful noise came from the control tower. It was Ignatius laughing and starting the countdown to liftoff.

Super-Turtle had to free his cat pal  — and fast.

"Hang on, Streaky!" Super-Turtle called. Streaky moved his head slightly but didn't open his eyes.

"I hope your feline friend likes the water, Super-Turtle," Ignatius shouted into a microphone. "It's a long swim back from where he's headed!"

The countdown continued.

The rocket was aimed at a top-secret island in the middle of the ocean. With his superpowers weakened, Streaky would be stuck at sea forever!

 "Not so fast!" shouted Super-Turtle. The hero sped toward the high-tech rocket, hoping to save his friend.

WHAM-O! Super-Turtle suddenly fell to the ground like a stone.

"Hahaha!" Ignatius laughed. "That kitty carrier is made of pure kryptonite. Kryptonians are powerless against it!"

Ignatius was right. Kryptonite could make anyone from the planet Krypton as weak as a noodle. However, there was one thing Ignatius didn't know . . .

Streaky wasn't from Krypton!!

Supergirl had created Streaky during an experiment with X-kryptonite. It was the only thing that gave the Super-Cat superpowers.

Super-Turtle could do only one thing. To save Streaky, he needed to reverse the power of the Sleepy-Time Sauce. He needed something that was right under their feet — **X-kryptonite!**

Before the clock could count down any further, Super-Turtle took off. He zoomed straight up into the air, faster than a rocket.

Then, pausing just inside the Earth's atmosphere, he turned and aimed.

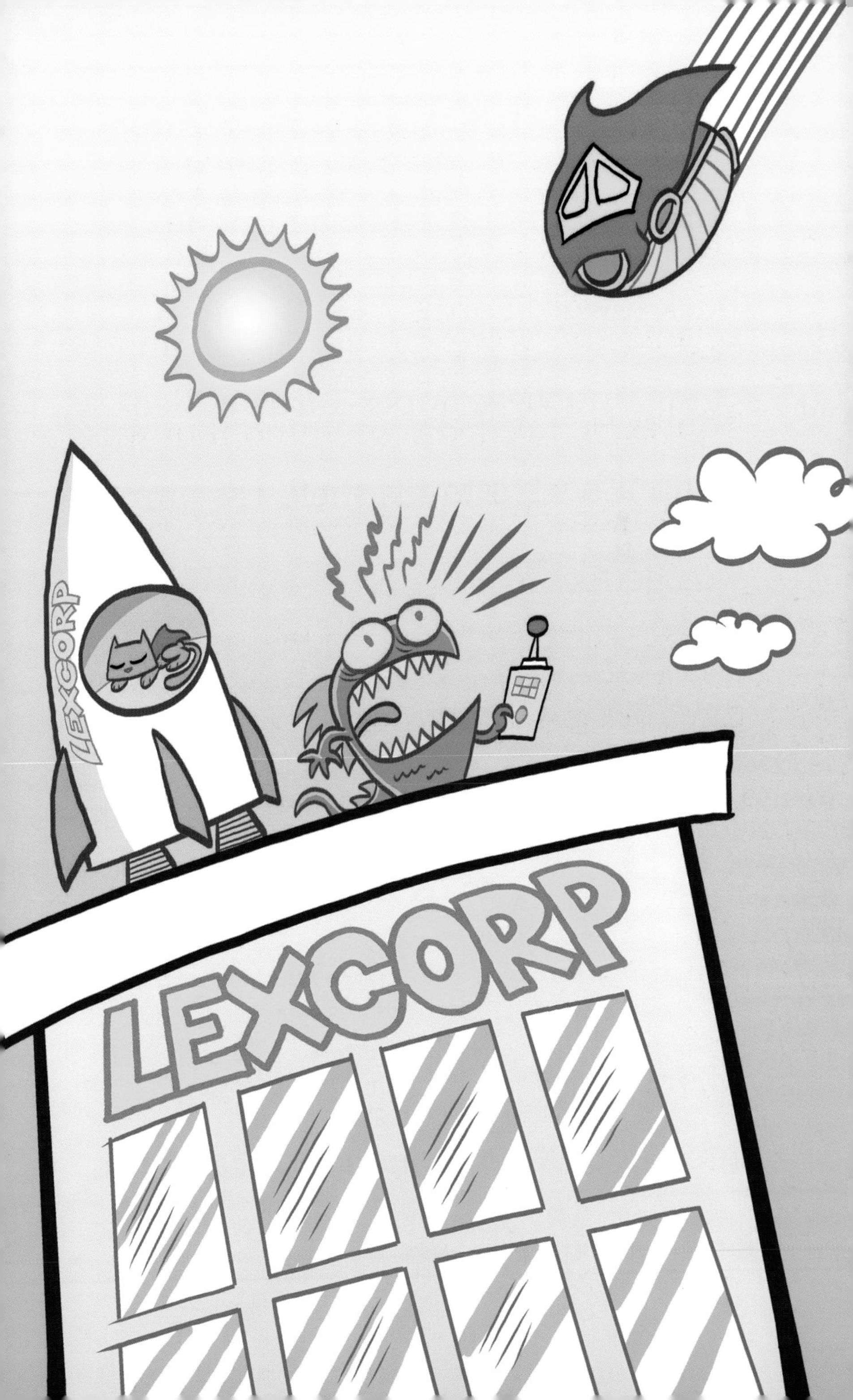
LEXCORP
LEXCORP

The clock ticked down the seconds as Super-Turtle hurtled faster and faster back toward Earth. As the rooftop came into view, Super-Turtle pulled himself back into his shell. His aim was perfect.

Super-Turtle smashed through the walls of LexCorp as if they were made of paper. He tore through concrete and steel. At last, he blasted the target: a safe full of X-kryptonite that LexCorp kept for experiments.

4ooo3ooo

The X-kryptonite's green glow

reached Streaky just in time. It reversed

the effects of the Sleepy-Time Sauce.

The old Streaky was back! But now,

Super-Turtle was in trouble.

SMASH!!

At full strength, Streaky broke free of the kryptonite kitty carrier. He needed to help restore Super-Turtle's powers, just as his friend had helped him.

"You could use a good tan," Streaky said, patting Super-Turtle's shell.

ZOOO

"Rocket is ready for liftoff," a mechanical voice reported.

Streaky shoved his weakened friend inside the rocket. But not to get rid of him. After a few hours in the island sun, Super-Turtle would be back.

"Not so fast!" shouted Ignatius Iguana. He grabbed Streaky, wrestling with the Super-Cat atop the rocket.

"Chill out, Ignatius!" said Streaky. He blasted the evil iguana with freeze breath as the rocket roared to life.

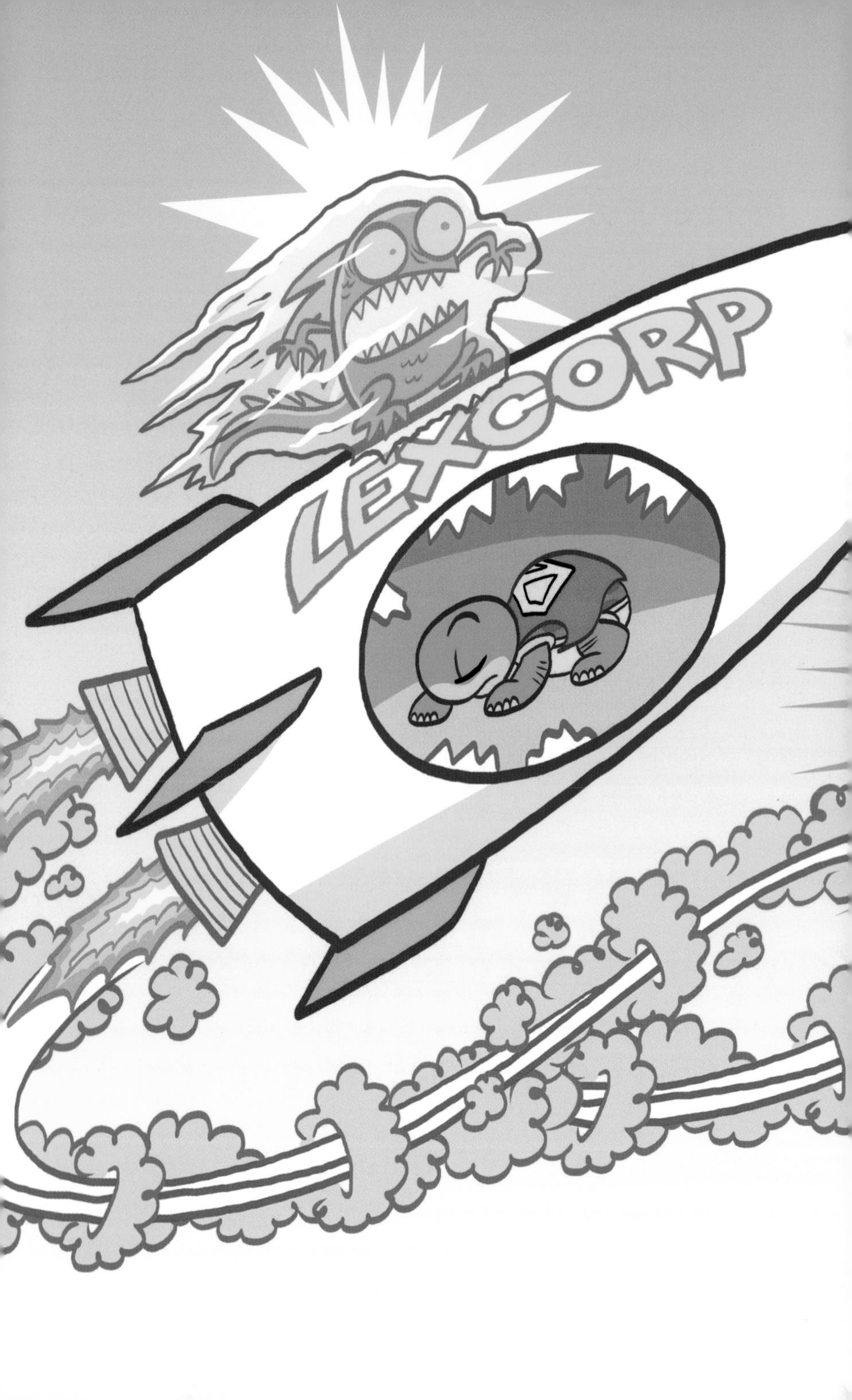
LEXCORP

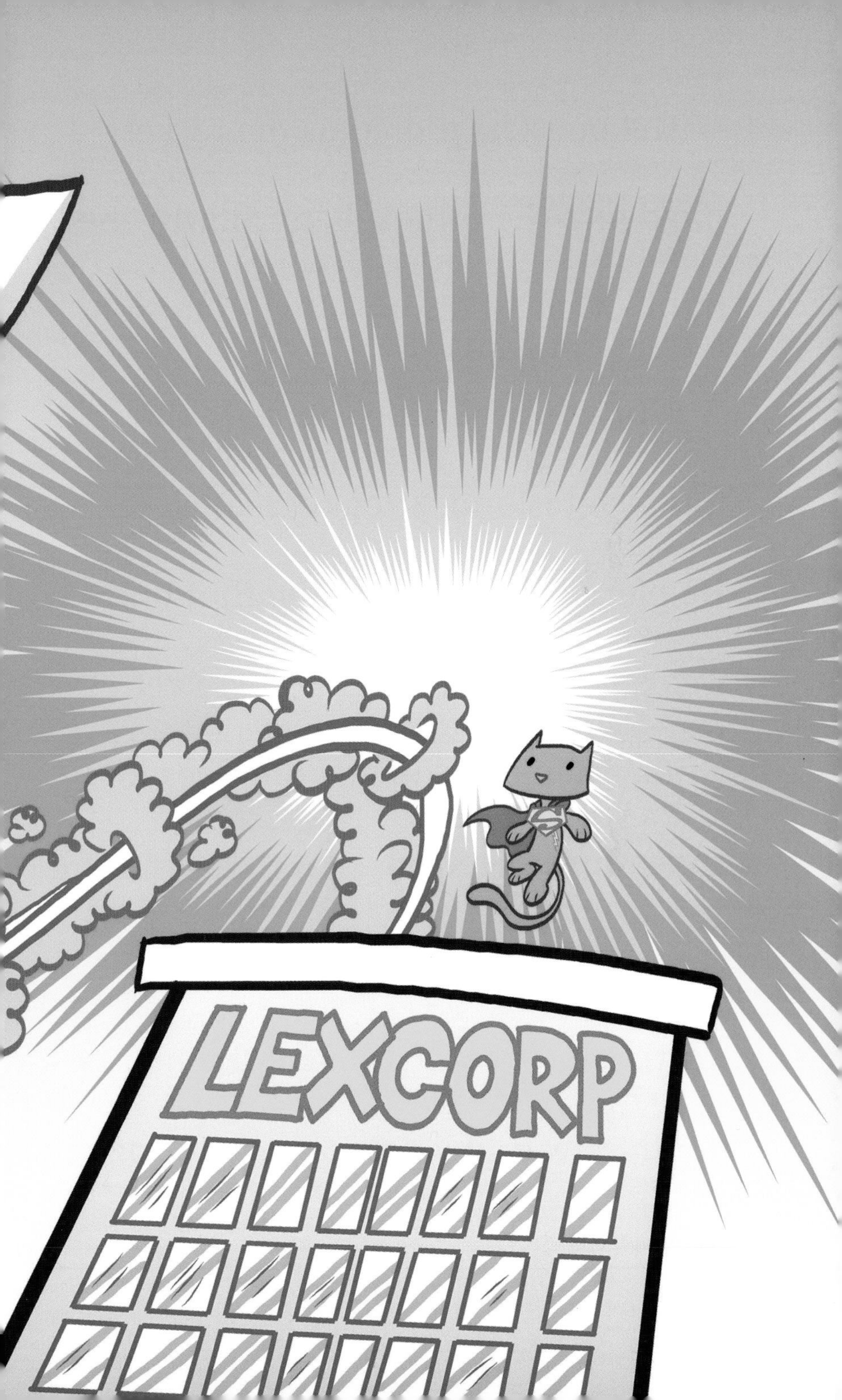
LEXCORP

The boosters roared as the rocket lifted into the atmosphere. Slowly, the hunk of metal disappeared from sight.

While Super-Turtle soared to the top-secret island, Streaky cleaned up. He placed the X-kryptonite that had weakened his friend in a top secret vault. Then he searched the skies for Super-Turtle's return.

Minutes passed, and Streaky was starting to get a little worried. Then he finally saw a tiny green speck in the wide blue sky.

WOOOOSH!

People shouted and pointed.

It was Super-Turtle! He was back

to full strength and ready to go!

Streaky had never been so happy to see Super-Turtle before. "Thanks for saving me," he said.

"Thanks for saving *me*," Super-Turtle replied. "And thanks for sending Ignatius on a much-needed vacation!"

"**I hope that old iguana packed sunscreen,**" Streaky said.

"I don't think it will matter," Super-Turtle replied. "**Ignatius has already been burned.**"

END!

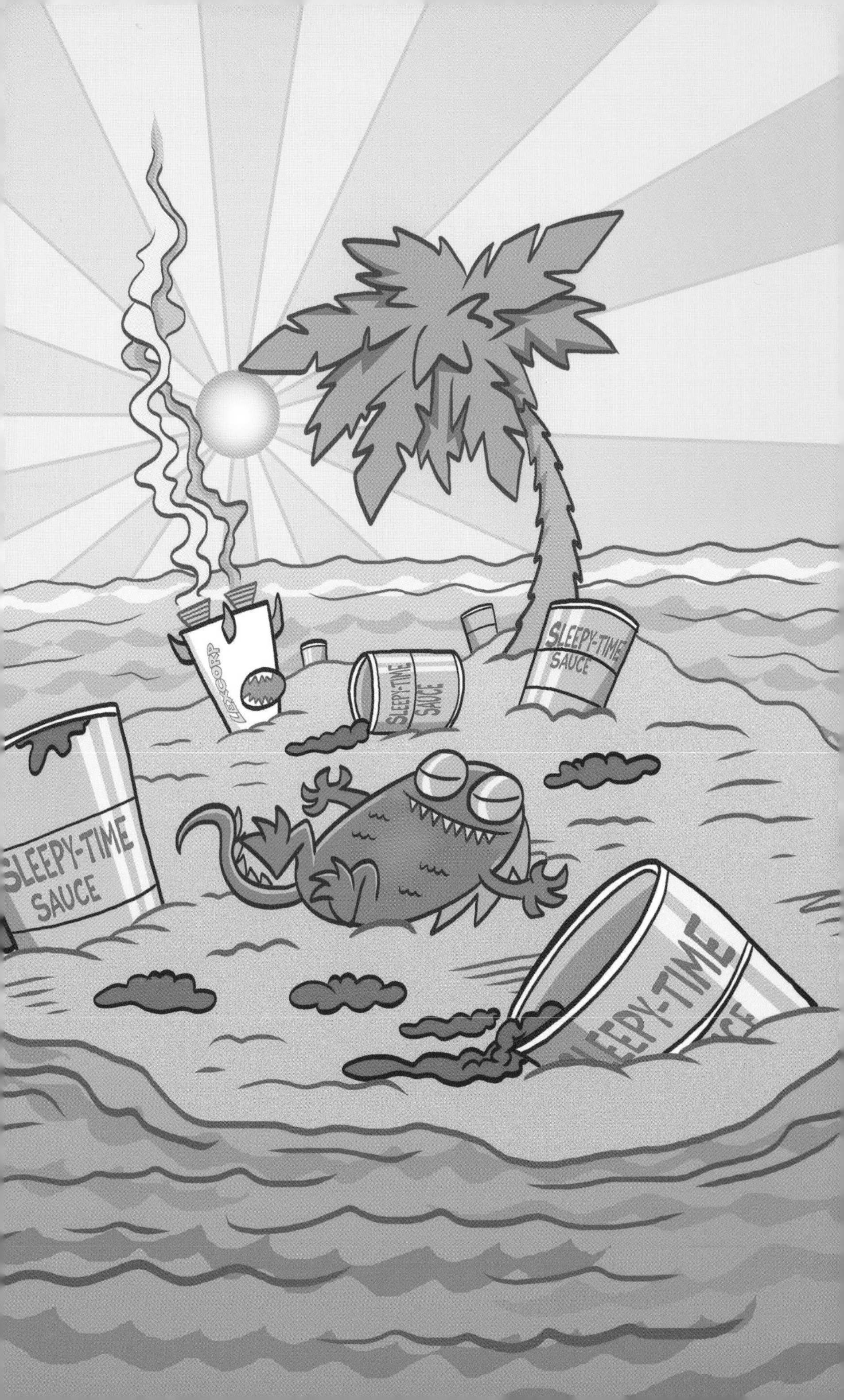
LEXCORP
SLEEPY-TIME SAUCE
SLEEPY-TIME SAUCE
SLEEPY-TIME SAUCE

KNOW YOUR HERO PETS!

1. Krypto
2. Streaky
3. Beppo
4. Comet
5. Super-Turtle
6. Fuzzy
7. Ace
8. Robin Robin
9. Batcow
10. Jumpa
11. Whatzit
12. Hoppy
13. Storm
14. Topo
15. Ark
16. Fluffy
17. Proty
18. Gleek
19. Big Ted
20. Dawg
21. Paw Pooch
22. Bull Dog
23. Chameleon Collie
24. Hot Dog
25. Tail Terrier
26. Tusky Husky
27. Mammoth Mutt
28. Rex the Wonder Dog
29. B'dg
30. Sen-Tag
31. Fendor
32. Stripezoid
33. Zallion
34. Ribitz
35. Bzzd
36. Gratch
37. Buzzoo
38. Fossfur
39. Zhoomp
40. Eeny

1

2

3

4

5

6

7

8

9

10

11

12

13

14

15

16

17

18

19

20

21

22

23

24

25

26

27

28

29

30

31

32

33

34

35

36

37

38

39

40

KNOW YOUR VILLAIN PETS!

1. Bizarro Krypto
2. Ignatius
3. Brainicat
4. Mechanikat
5. Crackers
6. Giggles
7. Joker Fish
8. Rozz
9. Artie Puffin
10. Griff
11. Waddles
12. Mad Catter
13. Dogwood
14. Chauncey
15. Misty
16. Sneezers
17. General Manx
18. Nizz
19. Fer-El
20. Titano
21. Mr. Mind
22. Sobek
23. Bit-Bit
24. X-43
25. Starro
26. Dex-Starr
27. Glomulus
28. Rhinoldo
29. Whoosh
30. Pronto
31. Snorrt
32. Rolf
33. Squealer
34. Kajunn
35. Tootz
36. Eezix
37. Donald
38. Waxxee
39. Fimble
40. Webbik

MEET THE AUTHOR!

Sarah Hines Stephens

Sarah Hines Stephens has authored more than 60 books for children and written about all kinds of characters, from Jedi to princesses. When she is not writing, gardening, or saving the world by teaching about recycling, Sarah enjoys spending time with her heroic husband, two kids, and super friends.

MEET THE ILLUSTRATOR!

Eisner Award-winner Art Baltazar

Art Baltazar is a cartoonist machine from the heart of Chicago! He defines cartoons and comics not only as an art style, but as a way of life. Currently, Art is the creative force behind *The New York Times* best-selling, Eisner Award-winning, DC Comics series Tiny Titans, and the co-writer for *Billy Batson and the Magic of SHAZAM!* Art is living the dream! He draws comics and never has to leave the house. He lives with his lovely wife, Rose, big boy Sonny, little boy Gordon, and little girl Audrey. Right on!

WORD POWER!

caper (KAY-pur)—a criminal act, or a trick or prank

experiment (ek-SPER-uh-ment)—a scientific test to try out a theory or to see the effect of something

ingredient (in-GREE-dee-uhnt)—one of the items that something is made from, such as an item of a food recipe

kryptonite (KRIHP-tuh-nite)—a radioactive rock from the planet Krypton

prowl (PROUL)—to move around quietly and secretly

sub-zero (SUHB-ZIHR-oh)—any temperature below zero degrees

suspected (suh-SPEK-tid)—thought that someone was guilty with little or no proof

ART BALTAZAR SAYS:

HERO DOGS
GALORE!

SPACE CANINE
PATROL AGENCY!

KRYPTO THE
SUPER-DOG!

BATCOW!

FLUFFY AND THE
AQUA-PETS!

PLASTIC
FROG!

JUMPA
THE KANGA!

STORM AND THE
AQUA-PETS!

STREAKY
THE SUPER-CAT!

THE TERRIFIC
WHATZIT!

SUPER-TURTLE!

BIG TED
AND DAWG!

Read all of these totally awesome stories today, starring all of your favorite DC SUPER-PETS!

GREEN LANTERN BUG CORPS!

SPOT!

ROBIN ROBIN AND ACE TEAM-UP!

SPACE CANINE PATROL AGENCY!

HOPPY!

BEPPO THE SUPER-MONKEY!

ACE THE BAT-HOUND!

KRYPTO AND ACE TEAM-UP!

B'DG, THE GREEN LANTERN!

THE LEGION OF SUPER-PETS!

COMET THE SUPER-HORSE!

DOWN HOME CRITTER GANG!

Picture Window Books™

Published in 2013
A Capstone Imprint
1710 Roe Crest Drive
North Mankato, MN 56003
www.mycapstone.com

Copyright © 2017 DC Comics.
[CHARACTER NAME] and all related characters and elements © & ™ DC Comics.
WB SHIELD: ™ & © Warner Bros. Entertainment Inc. (s18)

STAR25287

Cataloging-in-Publication Data is available at the Library of Congress website.
ISBN: 978-1-4048-6485-6 (library binding)
ISBN: 978-1-4048-7215-8 (paperback)

Summary: When Streaky won't wake from his catnap, his friend Super-Turtle discovers something shell shocking. The Super-Cat's kibbles are filled with an evil ingredient, and Ignatius Iguana is to blame. Can Super-Turtle nab this vile reptile before it's too late, or will Streaky be forever sleepy?

Art Director & Designer: Bob Lentz
Editor: Donald Lemke
Creative Director: Heather Kindseth
Editorial Director: Michael Dahl

Printed and bound in the United States of America.
032018 000342

DC SUPER-PETS!™

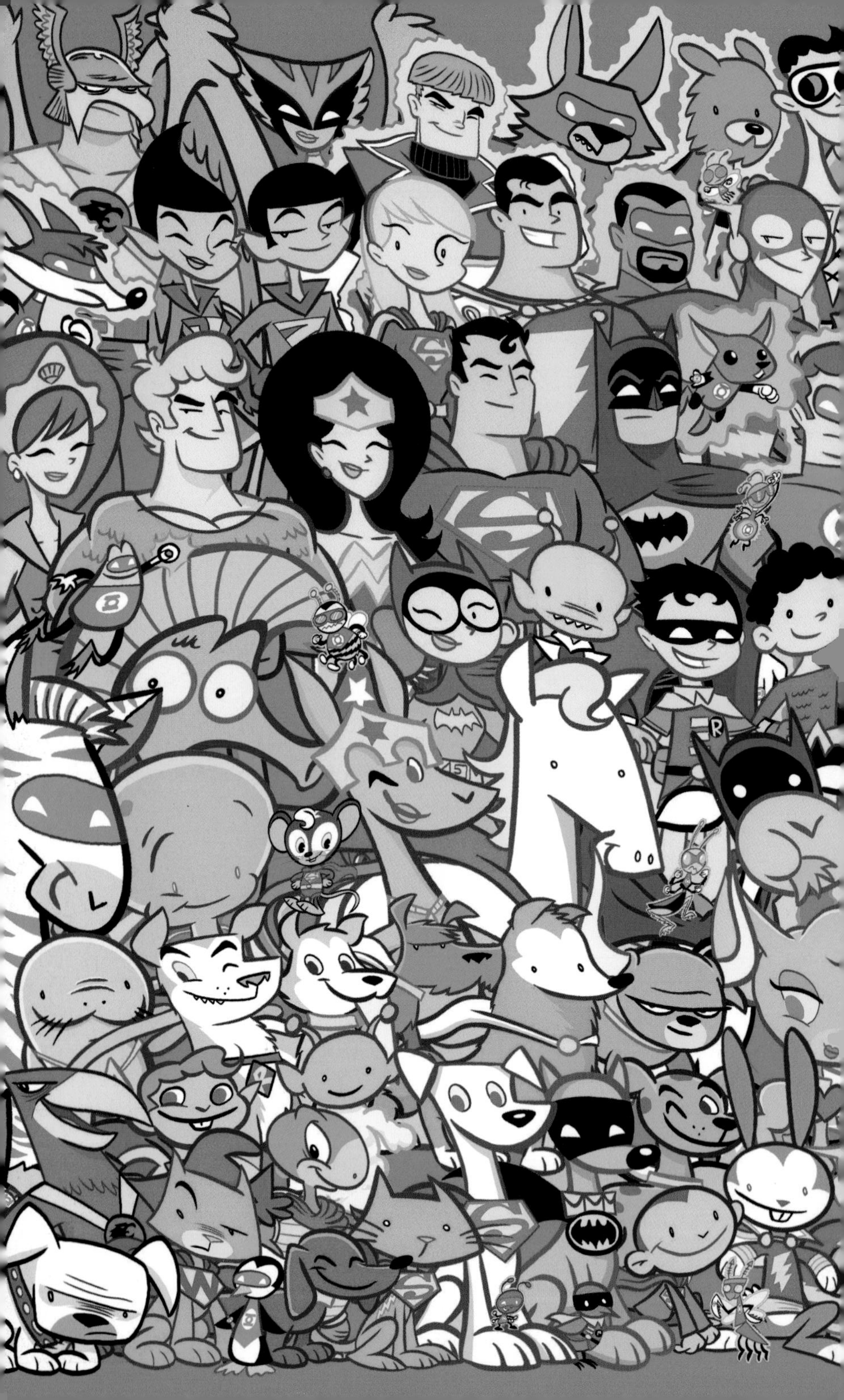